Getting from place to place in my community

Bobbie Kalman

Crabtree Publishing Company
www.crabtreebooks.com

Created by Bobbie Kalman

For Aiden Salter,
who likes music, Flash, and Spiderman,
and loves swimming in his Grandma and
Grandpa's pool in the Bahamas

Author
Bobbie Kalman

Editor
Kathy Middleton

Educational consultants
Jennifer King
Janine Deschenes

Photo research
Bobbie Kalman

Design
Bobbie Kalman
Katherine Berti
Samara Parent (cover)

Print and production coordinator
Katherine Berti

Illustrations
Barbara Bedell: p. 20–21, 23 (tl)
Jeanette McNaughton-Julich: p. 21 (cr)

Photographs
iStock: ktaylorg: p. 6 (br)
Shutterstock: Arina P Habich: p. 5 (bl); Rob Wilson: p. 7 (bl); Flik47: p. 12 (b); Jaroslav Moravcik: p. 13 (br); Thomas La Mela: p. 13 (t); Luis Carlos Torres: p. 14 (bl); Daniel M. Silva p. 14 (bkgd); Javen: p. 17 (tr)
Thinkstock: p. 21 (br)
Cover and all other images by Shutterstock

Library and Archives Canada Cataloguing in Publication

Kalman, Bobbie, author
Getting from place to place in my community / Bobbie Kalman.

(My world)
Includes index.
Issued in print and electronic formats.
ISBN 978-0-7787-9596-4 (hardcover).
ISBN 978-0-7787-9604-6 (softcover).
ISBN 978-1-4271-1977-3 (HTML)

1. Transportation--Juvenile literature. 2. Vehicles--Juvenile literature. I. Title. II. Series: My world (St. Catharines, Ont.)

HE152.K32 2017 j388 C2017-905160-1
C2017-905161-X

Library of Congress Cataloging-in-Publication Data

Names: Kalman, Bobbie, author.
Title: Getting from place to place in my community / Bobbie Kalman.
Description: New York : Crabtree Publishing Company, (2018) | Series: My world | Includes index.
Identifiers: LCCN 2017053517 (print) | LCCN 2017055904 (ebook) | ISBN 9781427119773 (Electronic HTML) | ISBN 9780778795964 (reinforced library binding : alk. paper) | ISBN 9780778796046 (pbk. : alk. paper)
Subjects: LCSH: Transportation--Juvenile literature.
Classification: LCC TA1149 (ebook) | LCC TA1149 .K35 2018 (print) | DDC 388--dc23
LC record available at https://lccn.loc.gov/2017053517

Crabtree Publishing Company
www.crabtreebooks.com 1-800-387-7650

Printed in the U.S.A./022018/CG20171220

Published in Canada
Crabtree Publishing
616 Welland Ave.
St. Catharines, Ontario
L2M 5V6

Published in the United States
Crabtree Publishing
PMB 59051
350 Fifth Avenue, 59th Floor
New York, New York 10118

Published in the United Kingdom
Crabtree Publishing
Maritime House
Basin Road North, Hove
BN41 1WR

Published in Australia
Crabtree Publishing
3 Charles Street
Coburg North
VIC 3058

Contents

From here to there	4
Kinds of transportation	6
Getting to school	8
Outdoor fun	10
City traffic	12
Living near water	14
Up and down mountains	16
Winter challenges	18
Travel long ago	20
Where on Earth?	22
Words to know and Index	23
Notes for adults	24

From here to there

Each day, most of us go from one place to another in or near our **communities**. Communities are the places where we live. Sometimes we travel to places that are far away, but most of our trips are close to our homes. Where do you go in your community?

Getting around

We use **transportation** to get from place to place. Transportation is how we move people and things from one place to another. What are the main ways that you get around your community? Do you walk, take a bus, ride a bike, or get a lift in a car?

Does your family have a car? How many people can fit in it?

Do you have an amusement park near you? What is your favorite ride?

How do you get to your doctor or dentist?

Kinds of transportation

A few kinds of transportation that you may have in your community are shown on these pages. Some transport people, and some carry **goods**, such as food, furniture, or tools.

Taxis are cars that transport people from place to place. People pay for the ride.

This moving truck is carrying a family's belongings from one home to another.

Wheelchairs transport people who cannot walk.

Airplanes transport people and goods to places far away.

Helicopters are small aircraft that fly using spinning **rotors**.

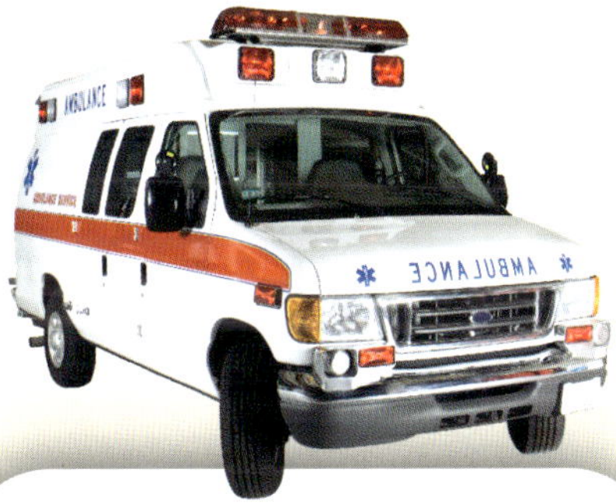

Ambulances carry sick people to a hospital.

Trains run on tracks of steel. This train is called a **trolley** or streetcar.

Fire trucks carry firefighters and equipment to put out fires.

What is your favorite way of getting around in your community?

Getting to school

If you do not live close to a school in your community, you may have to take a bus to school and back home again. These children are ready to go home. Their teacher makes sure they get on the school bus safely.

How do you get to school?

Children who live close to their school can walk or ride a bike or scooter. Those who live farther away might take a bus or be driven to school by an adult. How do you get to school?

Does someone walk or drive you to school?

Outdoor fun

There are many ways of getting around that are good for exercise or just for having fun. Do you have parks near where you live? Parks are fun places to walk your dog, ride your bike, or have fun running around with your friends or family. How do you get to your favorite park? Are you close enough to walk or ride your bike, or does someone have to drive you?

Some parks have lanes for joggers, bikes, or scooters.

There's a lot of room in a park for running around with your friends or your dog.

Are there woods near you that have bumpy trails for mountain bikes?

Many families go for hikes or camping trips. Have you ever slept in a motorhome? Tell a friend about your camping trip.

City traffic

People who live in cities have several ways of getting around. Most city streets today are crowded with **traffic** such as cars, buses, and taxis. People also take trains, streetcars, and **subways** to get to where they need to go. Streetcars move on tracks found on city streets, and subways are trains that move under the ground. If you live in a city, how do you get to the places you need to go?

My mother and I take the subway to visit family or go to the mall.

In cities, many people walk from place to place. Some ride motorcycles.

Many city streets now have lanes just for bikes. Does your city or town have bike lanes?

Living near water

Many people who live near water move from place to place by boat. Some people take a **ferry** to school or to work. A ferry is a boat that carries people and cars across water. Some ferries transport people to nearby islands for a day of fun.

Some people use motorboats to get from place to place quickly on water.

These pictures show many fun ways to move around on a lake or river. Which of these ways have you tried?

Up and down mountains

Mountains are areas of rocky land that rise high above the ground. Roads on mountains can be steep and winding, making driving difficult and slow. Are there mountains near your home? How do you get up and down a mountain?

*Skiers take a **ski lift** up to the top of a mountain...*

...then have fun skiing all the way down. Have you ever skied?

An easy way to get up and down mountains is in railway cars like these, which are pulled along tracks on mountains.

If you live near a mountain, do you hike in summer and toboggan, snowboard, or go skiing in winter?

This family is climbing a mountain. Climbing is great exercise!

Winter challenges

In many places, winter means a lot of snow and ice! Getting around is not fun for people who have to drive cars on icy roads or walk on slippery sidewalks.

Cars traveling on icy roads must drive more slowly for safety.

Machines that remove snow are used to clear roads and sidewalks.

Snow days

Skiing, tobogganing, and skating are some fun ways to get around in winter. Some families prefer to take a break from the cold. They fly to a warm place instead for a vacation!

Skating on a frozen pond or river is lots of fun!

What will this boy do on his vacation? How do you know?

This girl is having fun with dolphins on her vacation. What would you like to try if you could go to a warm place on vacation?

Travel long ago

Long ago, there were no cars, trucks, or airplanes. On land, wagons and carts pulled by horses or oxen were used to carry heavy loads. Horses also pulled **carriages** that carried people from place to place.

Oxen pulled this wagon filled with heavy wood.

***Stagecoaches** were covered carriages that carried people from town to town. They also carried the mail.*

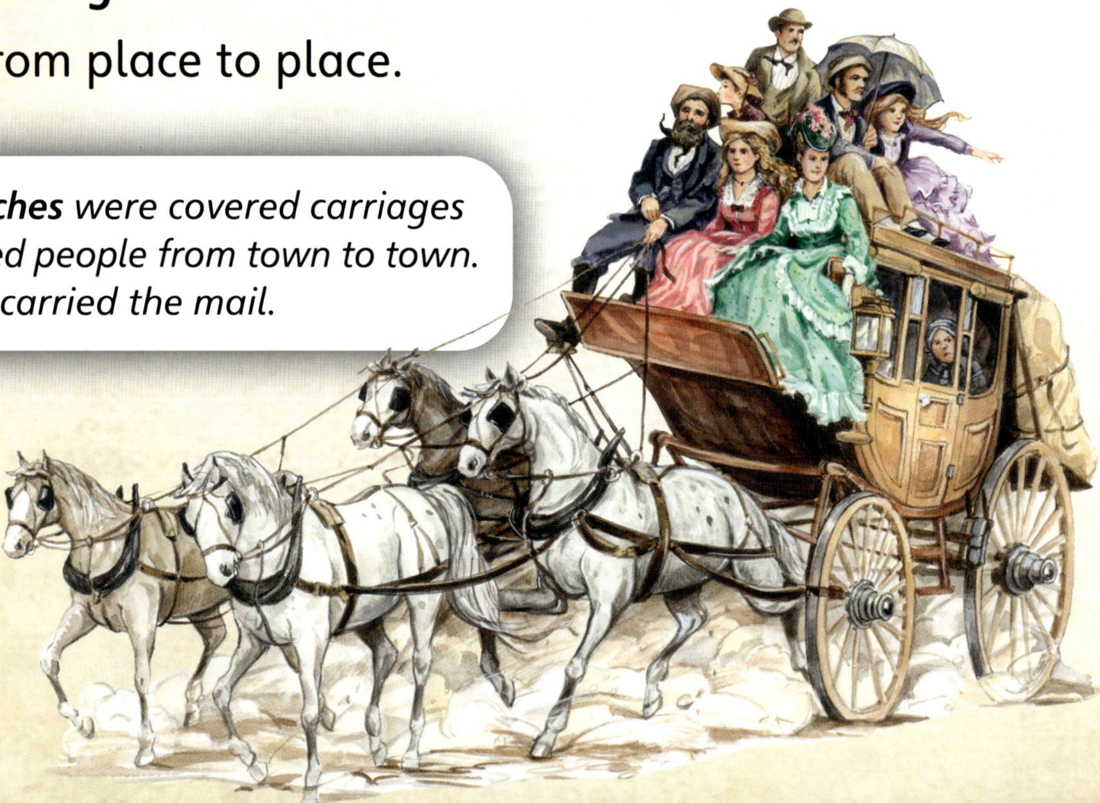

In winter, stagecoaches had **runners** instead of wheels to travel over snow.

Horses pulled boats along rivers and **canals**. Canals are waterways made by people.

A **high wheeler** was an early bicycle that had a large front wheel and a small back wheel. Its wheels were made of wood.

Steamships carried people across oceans.

Where on Earth?

This book is about getting around in your community, but today it is just as easy to travel around the world. There are so many kinds of transportation, that people can fly to the other side of the world in only a few hours. Helicopters can even land on the highest mountains. Soon, people will even go on vacations in space! With your friends, make a list of the places you would like to visit, including up in space!

How would each of you get to the places you want to go?

What would you like to do in each place?

Words to know and Index

animal transportation
pages 20–21

bicycles and motorcycles
pages 4, 5, 9, 10, 11, 13, 21

city transportation
pages 12–13

community transportation
pages 4–9

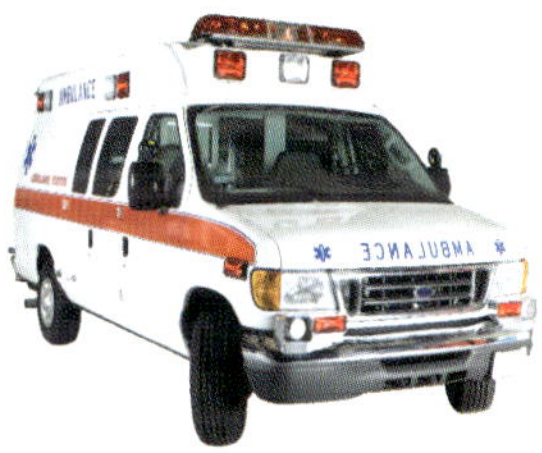

emergency transportation
page 7

flying
pages 7, 19, 22

mountain transportation
pages 16–17

winter transportation
pages 16–17, 18–19, 21

water transportation
pages 14–15, 21

Notes for adults

Objectives
- To teach children the different ways people get from place to place in their communities
- To introduce children to different kinds of communities that might require different methods of transportation
- To introduce nonfiction text features

Before Reading
- Read the title to the children and ask them what they think the book will be about.
- Scan the Contents list and discuss what they may learn from the book.
- Give the children sticky notes to jot down a few key words after they read each section.

During Reading
Ask the children:
- How do headings and captions help you?
- How do the photos help you understand the text? Which five photos do you like?
- Turn and Talk! Share with a reading partner an important detail you just read.

After Reading
- Using the Contents list, ask the children to elaborate on each section.
- Ask them to identify the big ideas in the text.
- Ask the children how transportation in the future may be very different from transportation today.

Discussion Points
- Ask the children in which kind of community they live. Invite them to list the main types of transportation there.
- Then ask them to share three methods of transportation that they most often use.

Yesterday and Today
Ask the children to compare transportation long ago to that of today.
- How were stagecoaches like buses? How were they changed in winter so they could travel on snow? How do cars travel on snow?
- How are bicycles different from the high wheelers of more than 100 years ago?
- Horses and oxen pulled wagons and coaches. What makes a car move?

Collaborative Writing
Invite children to write a letter to another class telling them what they learned from this book and why they should read it too.

Be a Reporter!
Guide children to choose their favorite type of transportation. Ask them to report facts about this method of transportation to the class by answering the following questions:
- What does it look like?
- How is it used?
- Does it have wheels, tracks, or wings?
- In which type of community is it used?
- Can it be found in every community?